THE RINK RATS

Irene Punt

illustrations by
Ramón Pérez

Scholastic Canada Ltd.
Toronto New York London Auckland Sydney
Mexico City New Delhi Hong Kong Buenos Aires

Scholastic Canada Ltd.
604 King Street West, Toronto, Ontario M5V 1E1, Canada

Scholastic Inc.
557 Broadway, New York, NY 10012, USA

Scholastic Australia Pty Limited
PO Box 579, Gosford, NSW 2250, Australia

Scholastic New Zealand Limited
Private Bag 94407, Botany, Manukau 2163, New Zealand

Scholastic Children's Books
Euston House, 24 Eversholt Street, London NW1 1DB, UK

Library and Archives Canada Cataloguing in Publication
Punt, Irene, 1955-
The rink rats / by Irene Punt ; illustrated by Ramón K. Pérez.

ISBN 978-1-4431-0442-5

I. Pérez, Ramón II. Title.

PS8581.U56R56 2010   jC813'.54   C2010-901828-1

6 5 4 3 2   Printed in Canada   121   13 14 15 16 17

MIX
Paper from
responsible sources
FSC® C004071

Contents

To Tom, Harty and Heather — with thanks
—I. P.

Rough Ice

"Awesome!"

"Wicked!"

Tom and his friends were inventing hockey plays Sunday afternoon at the outdoor rink at Crescent Park.

The puck passed from Tom to Stuart to Tom to Mark.

THWACK! Mark took a shot on net.

BAM! Jordan punched the puck with his goalie blocker. It rebounded. Tom grabbed the puck with his stick and fired a shot. "Goal!" he shouted, raising a fist.

Jordan made his scary goalie face and everyone laughed.

"Let's do that passing play one more time!" said Tom. "It's like a pinball machine! *PING PING PING!*"

"Hold it!" announced Stuart excitedly. "Let's call this play The Pinball!"

"Yaah!" Everyone agreed with a high-five. All together they shouted out their hockey team's name — "Glenlake Hawks!"

Jordan grabbed his water bottle and took a big squirt. He lowered his goalie mask. "I'm ready."

Stuart skated backwards. He wobbled and fell. "Not again!" he complained.

Tom looked at the ice. It was rough — full of bumps, cracks and chunks. His skates and his teeth ch-ch-ch-ch-chattered to the centre of the rink, but he kept his balance. "We gotta do something about this." Then he caught sight of a snow shovel. "You guys keep going. I'm going to start scraping!"

Tom pushed hard on the shovel, thrusting

it back and forth across the ice. *SKWYCH! SKWYCH! SKWYCH!* Finally, a stubborn piece of ice broke loose and he flicked it into the snow. "Woo hoo!"

"What are you doing?" asked Stuart.

"Fixing our rink." Tom didn't look up. He grunted, "Unh!" as he grated. *SKWYCH! SKWYCH!* "Yay!" he cheered. "I just flattened the bump Stuart tripped on!"

"Tom thinks he's a Zamboni," whispered Mark.

"Zamboni, baloney!" said Tom, flexing his muscles. "These arms are made to shovel! Watch this . . ." He powered up and worked faster. "Cool!" Another section of ice was smooth.

Mark, Stuart and Jordan stopped skating. Tom seemed to be having more fun than they were.

Stuart positioned his stick next to a lump of crusty snow and joined in. "I'm gonna scrape away this blob!" he said.

"Me too!" said Mark, with a wallop of his stick. "Look! I just got rid of a whopper ice cube!"

Finally, Jordan took off his goalie blocker. "Grrmph!" He revved up.

The boys worked and worked on the ice until . . . *BLEEP! BLEEP!* rang Stuart's walkie-talkie. He pulled it out of his pocket and glanced at his house, across from the park. His mom was at the window, waving her walkie-talkie. "Time to come home!" she told him.

Stuart pressed the talk button. "Hey, Mom. We're kinda busy doing rink improvements!"

"You've got two more minutes!" she said. "Then home!"

"Oh, rats! Let's scrape faster!" said Mark. "This is fun!"

"Rats? Hey, good one, Mark!" Tom laughed. "We're rink rats, like the kids who help out at the arenas!"

Everyone howled.

Five minutes later, Tom studied the rink. It looked bigger. And better. He skated one quick lap, cruised by the net, turned and glided backwards. "Wow! This ice is nice! Check it out!"

The four boys skated back and forth, forward and backwards, while Mark sang, *"Our rink ain't gonna stink no more, no more!"* They raised their hands and slapped a round of high-fives.

BLEEP! BLEEP! Three walkie-talkies blared at the same time.

"Get home, quick!"

"Dinner!"

"You have a game!"

"Uh-oh, it's Game Night! Let's go!" said Tom.

Game Night

Centennial Arena rocked with spectators. Tom strained forward in the players' box, his eyes on the scoreboard. It was now the third period with two minutes remaining. The Woodland Warriors were winning 2–1. *Come on, Hawks! We can do it!* Tom told himself.

Coach Howie rattled the gate for a line change after an icing call. Three tired skaters headed for the bench.

"Mark. Stuart. Tom. You guys are on!" Coach Howie said, as he tipped his Hawks cap.

"Go, Hawks, go!" yelled the fans.

Mark and Stuart positioned themselves, while Tom set up at the faceoff spot. The linesman dropped the puck. Tom fought for it and lost. As Warrior #2 picked up the pass, Stuart skated hard, reached out his stick and stole the puck. He raced up the ice.

"Pinball," Tom said. "Pinball!"

The puck passed from Stuart to Mark to Tom — over and over as the Warriors goalie shifted up and down, side to side. Then Tom whacked the puck, and it flew into the net.

"The Pinball worked!" Tom whooped.

"Yahoo!" the team howled.

The score was now 2–2.

Again, they set up at centre ice. This time Tom won the faceoff. He tapped the puck to Mark. Mark sent it back to Tom. He caught the pass and took off. *ZOOM!*

The Warriors' winger charged after Tom, swiping at the puck. "Whoops!" cried the winger. His glove and stick went flying. They hit the ice and skimmed across it, blocking Tom's path.

"Oh, no!" gasped the fans.

Tom skate-stepped over the stick. And the glove. His strides were powerful. His eyes stayed focused on the goalie. *THWACK!* He took a shot. The puck soared into the net.

"Yeah!" cheered the Hawks' fans.

"Woo hoo!" shouted the team.

Tom raised his fist as the clock sounded: *BUZZZZ!* The game was over. It was 3–2 for the Hawks.

As Tom lined up to shake hands with the Warriors, he thought, *Skating over obstacles is nothing after shinny on rough ice!*

For the Team

Coach Howie stood in the centre of the dressing room. Fifteen sweaty Hawks sat on the benches around him. "Great game tonight!" he announced. "Tom's fancy footwork was awesome!"

Tom liked his coach. He liked his team. It felt good when he made them happy.

"Now, listen up! I know it's late, but I have an announcement," said Coach Howie. "We weren't able to get an ice time here for our upcoming Family Day game."

"What?"

"Bummer!"

Everyone was disappointed.

"Maybe we could do something different." Coach Howie looked hopeful. "Any ideas?"

"But playing hockey against our families is the best!" said Ben.

"How about . . ." blurted Tom, "we have the game at an outdoor rink?"

Everyone perked up.

"There's one in our neighbourhood that could work," he said, his heart pounding with excitement.

"But most outdoor ice is really bad," said

Spencer. "It's like skating on crunchy peanut butter."

Tom signalled his friends for support.

"Hey, no worries," said Mark, spreading his arms. "This rink is smooooooooth!" Stuart and Jordan nodded.

"It's as good as the Saddledome!" Tom added.

"Wow!" Everyone seemed impressed.

"Gee, thanks, boys! This is excellent news!" Coach Howie looked at the team. "I

guess the Family Day game is on! Invite the whole gang!"

"YAY!" Everyone cheered till Tom's ears buzzed.

"Now, who wants to help with food, music or decorations? There are lots of jobs to do!" Coach Howie passed around a sign-up sheet.

— ● —

As Tom, Stuart, Mark and Jordan carried their hockey bags down the long hallway, Mark mumbled, "Oh, man. Our rink's not *that* good."

"Not as good as the Saddledome!" Stuart gulped. "Yikes!"

"C'mon!" said Tom. "We've got two weeks. We can make the ice perfect."

"What if we can't?" asked Jordan. "The team will be mad at us."

"Hey, we're not going to let a few bumps

get in the way of our Family Day game!" said Tom.

"Okay," agreed his friends, banging their fists together.

"We can do this — for the team!" said Tom.

They slapped a round of high-fives, while Mark sang, *"Our rink ain't gonna stink no more, no more!"*

Tom's mom was standing beside the snack bar, talking to Jordan's and Mark's parents. The boys headed in their direction.

"Can we go to Crescent Park right now and work on the ice?" asked Tom.

"No!" the parents answered.

"But . . ."

"But . . ."

"NO!" repeated the parents.

Tom felt deflated. He had been all pumped up and ready to work. He waved goodbye to his friends and headed toward the car as a noisy snowplow scraped the parking lot.

"So, why can't I go to the rink?" Tom asked his mom.

"Because you need to be ready for school tomorrow," she answered.

"Huh?" *That's the weirdest reason in the history of the world*, Tom thought. He punched his hockey bag into the trunk.

Friendship

Monday, February 1.

Tom sat at his desk, colouring the new calendar page. It was titled *February Fun!*

"Did you know February is the shortest month?" announced Mark.

"Not good!" said Tom. "That means less hockey!"

Mrs. Wong, their teacher, stood at the front of the classroom. "We have a special day in February. Who knows the date?"

Stuart waved his hand. "Friday, February 12th! Everyone's going to wear red to the Calgary Flames game at the Saddledome. They're playing against Sidney Crosby!"

"Go, Flames!" said Mrs. Wong. "But I was thinking of something else."

"Our province has Family Day on February 15th," suggested Tom. "That's when our hockey team is going to play against our families." He looked around at his Hawks friends with a big grin. "I love scoring on my dad!"

"Go, Hawks!" said Mrs. Wong. "But, I was thinking of something else. Here's a clue." She held up a giant red heart. **LOVE** was printed across it.

"Valentine's Day!" said Amber. "February 14th!"

"That's it," said Mrs. Wong. "We'll have a party on the Friday before Valentine's Day — with cupcakes, games and a valentine exchange!" She put a star on the calendar. "Don't forget to wear something red *that* day!"

The girls smiled and nodded. Jordan rolled his eyes.

"Now, let's start decorating," said Mrs. Wong. She opened a large box and pulled out armfuls of paper doilies, hearts, cupids, roses, and lips. Some of the boys made kissing sounds, and all the girls giggled.

"Yecch!" Tom slid down in his seat. Mark choked. Stuart gagged.

"Oh, dear," said Mrs. Wong. "February might be the *longest* month." She looked at the decorations. "These things *are* a little sappy.

How about no mushy love stuff for Valentine's Day? Instead, let's make *friendship* our theme for February!"

A giant "WHEW!" filled the classroom.

Mrs. Wong continued. "Try making friendship cards for our valentine exchange. And you can work on a friendship project with your classroom buddies."

Tom looked at his three Hawks teammates. "For our project we can play hockey — and fix the rink!"

Mrs. Wong held up one hand. "The projects must be completed at school and they must demonstrate friendship."

Friendship is easy. February will be a no-brainer, thought Tom.

Shovelling

It was after school.

Tom stomped through a new fall of fluffy snow on the way to Stuart's house. Mark made a giant white puff of breath. "Brrrrr! My nose is frozen." He crossed his eyes to see if it was purple yet. It looked red.

"Grrmph," grumbled Jordan.

They knocked on Stuart's door. His sister, Kaitlyn, answered. "Hi," she said. "What's happening, dudes?"

"We need Stuart to ice-scrape with us," said Tom.

"Ice skate?" asked Kaitlyn. "I like to ice skate!"

"First things first," said Tom, holding up his shovel. "We promised to make our rink good for the Family Day hockey game!"

Stuart came around the side of the house with a shovel. They all tromped across his front yard, making fresh tracks. Mr. Watson, their neighbour, was slowly clearing his sidewalk. The boys looked at one another. All at the same time, they dropped their hockey equipment and put their shovels to work, up Mr. Watson's driveway and alongside his

house, removing the trampled-down snow.

"Wow! You guys plow like the trucks," chuckled Mr. Watson.

"We're just about finished." Tom pushed down extra hard. "Wow! You've got some stubborn spots!" he said, flipping the shovel blade to the other side to scrape. *SKWYCH! SKWYCH!*

BANG! BANG! Jordan bounced his shovel up and down like a jackhammer to break up the snow.

"I guess I left the snow for too many days and it got packed down solid," said Mr. Watson, red-faced. "Thanks for the help, boys. You saved my sore back."

"No problem!" said Tom. It felt good to help.

Mr. Watson said, "I saw you kids working on the rink yesterday."

"We're fixing the ice — for our hockey team," said Mark.

"You know, if you keep up the shovelling at the rink, I'll help you flood it," said Mr. Watson. "So start watching the weather. Flooding works best on a clear night, when the temperature is between minus ten and minus twenty." He pointed to the outside tap. "You can use water from my house and all my garden hoses."

"Cool!" said Tom, his eyes lighting up. "We'll keep shovelling!"

"We can use water from my house, too," added Stuart.

"I can't wait to watch water freeze!" said Mark.

Mr. Watson chuckled. "When you make it to the NHL, you can tell the fans all about your days of shovelling and outdoor rinks." He winked.

"We want to play for the Flames!" said Tom.

"Then you guys need to get going! Clear your ice and practise your shots!" said Mr. Watson.

The boys crossed the street and clomped through the snow, waving their shovels in the air, thoughts of playing in the NHL spurring them on.

"Attack!" shouted Tom, dumping his stick and skates and tilting his shovel at the edge of the rink. He pushed hard on the handle, marching forward with giant steps. The blade cut through the snow quickly and easily. Tom stopped and announced, "Hey, this feels like feathers compared to Mr. Watson's snow!"

"That's because we left the rink in good shape yesterday," said Stuart, zooming along with his shovel.

Ten minutes later, the boys were done and on to hockey — making up a new set of moves called The Pickle Play. An hour later, they sat on the bench, taking off their skates.

"I'm glad we volunteered to fix this ice," said Tom, looking at the rink.

"Ditto," said Mark.

"Ditto," said Stuart.

Jordan nodded.

"It makes me feel like a rink owner," said Tom. "Like this is our rink."

They all laughed.

"We're big-shot rink owners!" said Jordan.

"Hey, let's wear suits and ties on Family Day, like the NHL team owners do!" joked Mark.

Everyone cracked up.

As Tom walked home, he wondered: should he and his friends play in the NHL? Or should they own an arena? They both seemed like good ideas.

The Friends of Fred

Tuesday, February 2. Groundhog Day!

Tom sat at the art table, drawing a buck-toothed groundhog on his calendar.

"Psst," said Mark. "What about a Puck Hog Day? For all the hockey players who don't pass the puck!" He laughed at his own joke.

"*Shhh!*" said Mrs. Wong, turning up the radio. "Listen carefully."

The radio announcer boomed, "I'm here with Groundhog Fred at Foothills Farm. When Groundhog Fred came out of his burrow today, he saw his shadow and predicted . . . six more weeks of winter!"

"Six more weeks of outdoor hockey!" added Tom.

Kylie put up her hand. "How can a rodent forecast the weather?"

"Good question," said Mrs. Wong. "Any ideas?"

Mark said, "I think . . . because February is friendship month, Groundhog Fred has *friends* who help him with the prediction — like that radio guy."

"Good answer," said Mrs. Wong, as she signalled the laughter to stop.

"I didn't say anything funny," muttered Mark, blushing.

Suddenly, Tom had a mega brainwave. He caught Stuart, Jordan and Mark's attention.

"Hey, let's be Groundhog Fred's friends for our friendship project! Reporting the weather to our class will help everyone — especially the Hawks — because we need to watch the weather for our rink."

"Woo hoo! The four of us will *four*-cast the weather! Get it?" laughed Mark, holding up four fingers. "The Rink Rats help the rodent!"

A few minutes later, the boys gathered around the science table. Tom studied the five-day weather forecast in the newspaper. "Today is . . . mainly cloudy with flurries," he reported. "That means we might need to shovel the snow before our hockey practice."

Stuart checked the outside temperature on the thermometer. "It's zero," he said. "That's freezing. Good for ice. But not cold enough for flooding tonight."

At the end of the day, Mark announced to the class, "The Friends of Fred say: If you get zero on your spelling test, that's bad. But if you want *ice*, zero is good!"

"Happy shovelling!" added Tom.

Everyone laughed.

———•———

The next three days went exactly as predicted: snow, snow, snow, with lots of shovelling, shovelling, shovelling. Each day

the temperature dropped two degrees. The Friends of Fred gave these tips to the class:

Wednesday: Minus two degrees — Wear a tuque so you don't freeze your ears off.

Thursday: Minus four degrees — Don't leave your animals outside.

Friday: Minus six degrees — Check the emergency kit in the family car.

———— ● ————

Saturday. Minus eight and sunny. Game day!

Everyone wore sunglasses on their way to Centennial Arena.

At four o'clock, Tom stood at the spectator glass, watching the Zamboni pass through the gate. He waved at the driver.

"Zamboni, baloney!" hooted Mark, giving Tom a nudge. "Wait till tomorrow when it's minus ten! We're going to flood our rink like a bird bath!"

"Yaah!" Tom launched himself onto the ice with a powerful stride. *Ooo, this ice seems extra slippery,* he thought, trying to dig in his blades. And when he came in for a stop, his skates kept going. "Oh, no!" he gasped, sliding sideways into the Sunridge Sharks' team warm-up. *No edges!* But he controlled his knees and held his ankles strong.

The whistle blew. As the team headed for the players' box, Tom said, "We forgot to get our skates sharpened after all that outdoor hockey."

"I guess we're skating on spoons today," sighed Mark.

— • —

The first period was the hardest. But by the end of the third period, Tom had forgotten all about dull blades. He snatched the puck with his stick and blazed down the rink, while Stuart and Mark criss-crossed the ice to contain the Sharks' defenceman. *BAM!* Tom took a shot. The puck flew high and hit the glass with a thud.

Spencer tore after the puck, then dug it out of the corner. He popped it to Tom, in perfect position to score. Tom took a swipe, while his feet slipped away from him. He crashed down onto the ice and the puck skimmed right to a Shark.

"Yahoo!" cheered the Sharks fans.

Tom skated hard to the bench, with his head down.

"Shake it off," said Mark. "It's hard to win them all."

Coach Howie tipped his Hawks cap. Tom knew it was his secret way of saying, "Hang in there!"

Flooding

Sunday night. Minus ten!

Tom sat at the dinner table, eating a bowl of hamburger soup. "Wait till you see the rink, Dad!" he said. "It's awesome. We blasted off all the ice chunks, and got rid of the giant piles of snow that were blocking the edges." He visualized the Family Day game. "Our team is going to go crazy!" Tom downed a glass of milk, then stuffed a bun into his mouth.

"Slow down. What's the hurry?" asked Mom.

"Minus ten!" Tom answered. He and Dad gathered up their hockey equipment, boots, hats, gloves and a Thermos filled with hot chocolate. From the garage they got hoses and a nozzle.

— ● —

Crescent Park looked vacant. "It's really black at night," said Tom. The only brightness came from a distant street light and the moon. *I'm glad my dad's here*, he thought. Then his eyes adjusted to the dark.

Across the street, Mr. Watson opened his front door. "Something going on out there?"

HONK! HONK! blasted a horn. It was Mark and his dad. Tom waved. Mr. Boswell pulled their equipment bags out of the car.

"We're coming!" hollered Jordan and his older brother, Derek, making their way across the snow.

Stuart plodded to the edge of his yard. "Help!" He looked like a mummy wrapped in garden hoses. "These things are heavy!"

"Whoa!" said Tom's dad. "First the *family* team needs to practise — to get in shape for Family Day. After that, we'll flood the ice."

"Okay," said Stuart, untangling himself from the hoses. "I'll turn off the water."

———— ● ————

The Hawks set up the nets and, a few minutes later, they were circling the rink and making a plan. "Let's show these guys The Pickle Play," said Tom mischievously.

"Good one," whispered Mark. "My dad can't skate backwards."

"Be careful. Remember, Derek's good!" said Tom.

Jordan banged his stick on the pipes. "Let's go!"

Tom placed the puck at centre ice.

"It's hockey night at Crescent Park!" joked Mr. Watson, as he sat down on the bench.

The puck went end to end, was passed and

grabbed, over and over. Derek flicked it into the snow bank. "This rink needs boards!" he said, tossing the puck back into the game. Tom batted it down with a slash and a flick. *SWOOSH!* The puck soared into the net, top shelf.

"Yay!" cheered Mr. Watson.

Tom pumped his arm. "Finally!" Now the Hawks had two goals. The family team had three.

BLEEP! BLEEP! Stuart reached for his chest pocket and unzipped the zipper. He pulled out his walkie-talkie. "What?"

"Can I play?" Kaitlyn asked. He looked across the street. She was standing in the driveway, wearing a helmet and a pair of figure skates.

Stuart screwed up his face. "She's pretty bad."

Derek waved his arm in the air. "Kaitlyn . . . you're on our team! Come on!" Five minutes later, the score was 6–3 for the Hawks.

Tom stopped for a break. "Time to flood the rink?"

"Let's go!" cheered his friends.

As soon as their skates were off, the boys raced over to Stuart's house. But when they reached for the hose, they got a surprise.

"It's frozen solid!" gasped Stuart. There it sat on the lawn, like a giant pile of rock-hard spaghetti. "Sorry," he sighed. "I forgot about water freezing."

Mr. Watson emerged from his garage, pushing a hose cart. "Here are my garden hoses!" he said. "I've got a hundred metres."

"We brought some hoses, too," said Tom.

They connected them together, and then to the tap. Then they steered the stubborn hose cart across the road and through the snow to the edge of the rink. Stuart stayed back at Mr. Watson's. Tom paged him on his walkie-talkie. "Turn on the juice!"

Stuart turned on the tap.

"Yay!" Tom howled. He passed the hose to Mark to Jordan to Kaitlyn to Derek to Stuart — each spraying water onto the ice.

Suddenly a gust of wind whipped over the park, catching the mist and frosting them all. Tom's dad laughed. "You guys look like ice sculptures!" He took a picture with his cellphone.

As they drank hot chocolate, Tom stared at the rink. It was cool, watching water seep into the cracks and glaze over the scratches. By the time the hoses were put away, the ice looked as smooth and hard as a hockey helmet.

Wow! thought Tom. *We rule!*

Frustration

Monday. After school.

"Follow me," said Stuart, running toward home.

"Man, why do we have an early practice today?" complained Mark. "I want to skate on *our* rink — right now!"

"I bet the ice looks like glass," said Tom, puffed with excitement.

The boys turned the corner and saw the rink. "AAHHHHH!" they yelled. A bunch of girls was skating on it. Tom's heart was racing as he stomped across the snow. At the edge of the rink he gritted his teeth and took a cold, hard look at the surface. It was covered in scribbles and scratches.

"Hi, dudes," said Kaitlyn, skating up to them. She dug the picks of her figure skates into the ice.

"Uh . . . Kaitlyn . . . what are you doing?" gasped Stuart.

"Practising for Family Day," she said, chopping at a puck with one of her brother's sticks. Her friends skated by, pulling a sled full of Barbie dolls.

Mark choked. Jordan's mouth hung open. Tom was just about to throw his arms in the air and yell, when he saw Stuart's face. "Hey, Kaitlyn," he said instead. "Keep practising. The family team needs all the help it can get!"

Stuart looked up, relieved. "Right on!"

BLEEP! BLEEP! sounded a walkie-talkie. "Get home quick. You have a hockey practice!"

Tom hurried home. He needed to get his skates sharpened.

— • —

Centennial Arena.

"Skate backwards! Heads up!" hollered Coach Howie. Tom wove a figure-eight pattern around the orange cones, then glided to a stop behind Mark.

"Are you tired?" asked Mark.

"A little," said Tom.

Mark's face was white. He had dark circles under his eyes.

"I couldn't sleep last night," said Mark. "And I'm still freezing!" He scrambled towards the first cone.

"You're supposed to be skating backwards!" Coach Howie reminded him.

Mark spun around and wiped out. Hard.

Ouch! thought Tom. He skated over to help him up.

Coach Howie blew his whistle. "Okay, Hawks. Get into position for the next drill: The High-Speed Full-Ice Six-Pass Sideways Drill."

"Huh?" Stuart shook his head.

"Passes should be crisp!" added Coach Howie.

"Huh?" Mark frowned. "I don't get it."

Tom shut his eyes, trying to remember

everything Coach Howie had said. "It's like we're doing The Pinball." He took a deep, energizing breath. "Let's go."

Tom missed every pass. Mark missed every shot. Stuart missed his turn. And Jordan couldn't make a save. They were not crisp.

"What's with you guys? You're not even trying!" said Spencer. "This practice is important. Don't you care about the team?"

The words stung. Tom skated slowly to the players' bench and grabbed a water bottle. It wasn't fair. *Wait till they see the rink*, he thought. *We'll show them!*

—— ● ——

After practice, the dressing room was unusually quiet. Tom unlaced his skates and sat up, his back against the wall.

Coach Howie announced, "Spencer is Team Captain for our next game!" He gave

Spencer a big C to pin on his jersey while Tom held back his frustration.

Coach Howie said, "Team, you looked tired today. You fizzled out at the end. What if it had been a game?"

Mark mumbled, "The Hawks would be dead ducks."

Coach Howie nodded. "Remember, we play against the Tornadoes on Thursday. They are a strong, fast and smart team." He made eye contact with every player. "How can we prepare?"

"FERP!" said Tom, remembering their secret weapon.

Everyone joined in:

"F — Food!"

"E — Exercise!"

"R — Rest!"

"P — Practice!"

"And BE CAREFUL!" cautioned Coach Howie. "There are lots of bugs going around. Don't share your water bottles!" He looked at Mark. "What's your joke about water bottles?"

"Don't bug me!" everyone shouted.

Except Mark. He muttered, "Oops. I forgot."

Coach Howie finished up with, "We need to stay focused. We're not tweety birds, we are mighty . . ."

"Hawks!" everyone shouted.

Except Mark. He held his throat and squeaked a tiny, "Hawks!"

The boys hauled their hockey bags through the arena doors and headed for the ramp. "No stairs for me," rasped Mark. "I'm outta juice."

"Me too," admitted Tom, still trying to recover from Spencer's jab. "Good thing we've got our shovels to lean on when we fix the rink tonight."

Stuart blushed. "Sorry, man. I'm not allowed out tonight."

Jordan stammered, "I gotta make my friendship cards for the valentine exchange."

Mark opened his mouth, but nothing came out. He pointed to his throat.

"But . . ." Tom frowned. "We have to stay *focused* — on the rink!" His stomach lumped up like a frozen mitten. *We need to show the team how hard we work!*

You're Not Our Boss

It was Tuesday, after school. Mark was home, sick.

Tom, Stuart and Jordan marched to the rink, shovels over their shoulders, singing, *"Heigh-ho, heigh-ho . . . it's off to work we go!"*

Snow swirled across the ice, blowing around like flying laundry powder. Stuart frowned. "This dry snow is weird!"

They shovelled down the middle of the rink and around the outside. But when Tom looked up he saw mounds of snow. "What?" he sighed. "This is not working! I'm getting rid of the snow and you guys are putting it back!"

"You mean you're pushing the snow where I've already cleared," said Stuart, being defensive.

"I can't see any ice yet," complained Jordan.

"We need a plan," said Tom, frustrated. He thought hard. "Hey, what about snowplows? They clear at an angle." He positioned his shovel. "C'mon, join on."

Stuart and Jordan lined their shovels up with Tom's. Together they made a giant snowplow-like blade. Together they pushed forward, on an angle. They were almost done when a group of moms and little kids showed up to skate. "I guess we can't play shinny today," sighed Tom.

For a few minutes they watched the little kids charge around the smooth ice, playing happily. They didn't trip on ice chunks. They didn't fall on their faces. Tom felt good about that.

On Wednesday morning, there was a new layer of snow.

After school, Mark came to the rink dressed extra warm. He looked like a woolly marshmallow. "Our friend Fred forecasted winter and he was sooooo right!" he said. A small icicle hung from his runny nose.

Tom ordered, "Okay, guys, use the snowplow method."

Stuart rolled his eyes. "Don't tell us how to shovel. We know."

"No kidding," groaned Jordan, placing his shovel on an angle.

Tom showed Mark what to do.

As the boys pushed forward together, Tom

snapped, "Keep up to the guy next to you!"

"Oh, brother," sighed Mark.

— ● —

No one spoke during the game of shinny afterwards. As they were leaving, Tom said, "If it snows again, we'll shovel the rink right after school tomorrow, before our game against the Tornadoes."

"You're not our boss," said Jordan.

"I'm saving myself for the game," said Mark.

"But this rink needs *teamwork*," said Tom, totally discouraged. "Did you hear the word, *work*?"

"What's with you?" Stuart stood still. "Tom, you're forgetting the R in FERP! We need *rest* for tomorrow's game. We're half-dead."

Why are they acting like this? Tom wondered. *Family Day is a few days away!*

Without thinking, he blurted, "Don't you care about the Family Day game?"

"Whaaat?" Their eyes narrowed.

"We're all working hard!"

"Wait, guys!" said Tom, wanting to smooth things over. "You know what I mean."

Mark glared at Tom and mumbled quietly to himself, "Yup, you mean you're being mean."

Tom trudged home, worried about the rink and close to tears.

Fun and Games

Thursday, at school, Mrs. Wong displayed some friendship projects at the back of the classroom. Kylie and Amber made a paper chain, looping together words like Happiness, Laughter, Honesty, Compromise, Magic. Jadie and Taylor made a friendship dictionary. It was opened to KINDNESS.

Tom unrolled his group's poster. The title said:

We FOUR-cast the Weather with Groundhog Fred!

The top half was a drawing of the four Hawks, with their hockey sticks and shovels. Underneath, a list of weather tips was printed in felt pen. The latest tip was: **Happy shovelling! Don't let a little bump wreck your day!**

Tom thought about how he really liked being a Rink Rat with his friends. "Hey, guys!" he said. "Let's check out the weekend weather." But Mark, Stuart and Jordan didn't even look up. They stayed at their desks, working on their friendship cards.

"C'mon!" Tom pleaded. They were the only group not working together, and Mrs. Wong was watching. It felt weird — and lonely. He shivered, thinking about yesterday. *Why did I say they didn't care about the rink? Why did I have to be so bossy?*

Centennial Arena.

At six o'clock, the Hawks gathered around Jordan for their pre-game cheer. "Hawks! Hawks! Hawks!"

By the second period, the spectators were going crazy. The Tornadoes continued to storm the ice. Again and again their right winger breezed the zones, landing himself a hat trick. Stuart sucked in a deep breath. Jordan made his scary goalie face.

At 6:45 the score was tied at 3–3. Two players from the Tornadoes sat on their back bench, coughing and sneezing. Their power line was losing its zip.

"Go, Hawks, go!" yelled the Hawks fans.

"Blow, Tornadoes, blow!" yelled their fans.

WHEEE! The ref blew his whistle. The Tornadoes had too many men on the ice.

Bad luck for them, Tom said to himself. Now the Hawks would have a power play — five against four.

Tom said, "Let's try The Pickle." It was Stuart's favourite play.

Tom, Stuart and Mark got into position. The puck dropped at the faceoff circle. Tom batted the puck to Stuart. Stuart jumped at it, scooping the puck onto his blade. The Tornadoes zoomed after him. Too late. He

passed to Tom. Tom grabbed the puck, faked left, spun right and dodged a guy. Instead of shooting, he passed the puck to Mark. Mark flicked the puck as if he were flicking an ice chunk off his shovel. It whipped over the crouching goalie's head.

"Goal!" the ref called, pointing at the net.

Mark and Stuart celebrated with a glove punch. The score was now 4–3.

—— • ——

Ten minutes later, the Hawks were singing in their dressing room, *"We are the champions of the rink!"*

Coach Howie looked happy. "That game was a doozy! Great work, Hawks!"

"We just *blew* away the Tornadoes!" joked Mark. "We're not little birds in a windstorm!" He flapped his arms.

Everyone cheered, "We are the Hawks!"

"Don't forget — the Family Day game is

this weekend!" said Coach Howie. "It's going to be a ton of fun!"

Tom gulped nervously, trying to push the rink to the back of his mind.

Jack stood on the bench. "We've got a big-screen TV in our basement and the Flames play tomorrow night at the Saddledome. Who wants to watch the game at my house?"

"YAY!" The dressing room rocked. Mark and Stuart danced around.

Oh, man. Tom saw how excited his friends were. This was a sweet offer. And saying no would make him a party-pooper. Finally, he said, "Wow! Sidney Crosby! Better get there before the giant snowstorm hits the city!" Then he sat back. He kept a smile on his face, but inside he was worried.

Mark, Stuart and Jordan huddled together. "What about clearing the rink?" they whispered. They looked at Tom for direction. But he didn't look at them and he didn't say anything about it.

Staying
Focused

Friday, February 12.

"It's going to be a good Flames game!" said Jordan, on the way to school. "I can't wait!"

"And, look! No snow yet," said Mark.

"Yes. But . . ." Tom's lips twitched. He'd checked the barometer. The storm was on its way.

Stuart said, "Hey, no worries. We have all day Saturday and Sunday to whip the rink into shape."

They walked into the classroom. Everyone was wearing red.

"See?" said Mark. "Everyone is dressed for the Flames game tonight. *Everyone* will be watching it!"

"Go, Flames, go!" cheered Mark, Stuart and Jordan.

"We're wearing red for our Valentine's Day celebration," said Kylie, giggling.

———— ● ————

By lunchtime, snowflakes the size of popcorn were falling. *Oh, no,* thought Tom. He remembered how difficult it was to shovel the trampled-down snow on Mr. Watson's sidewalk. They really needed to shovel today. Not tomorrow. And if the snow was cleared away, they would have a chance to flood the rink before the game — maybe even twice. But Sidney Crosby was playing — their favourite NHL player!

———— ● ————

Mrs. Wong circled the classroom. She stopped next to the Hawks. They were busy colouring the picture on their friendship poster. "Good brainstorming! Look at all the helpful tips for bad weather!" She smiled. "It's a good thing you boys aren't just fair-weather friends."

"Huh?" The boys shook their heads. Sometimes Mrs. Wong said weird things.

— ● —

Mrs. Wong switched on the happy-face light. "It's party time!" She passed around a tray overflowing with chocolate cupcakes. "Have a snack, open your mailboxes and then we'll play bingo!"

Tom wolfed down his cupcake.

"Psst!" said Mark, with a chocolate smile. He held up the photo Tom had made into a friendship card. It was taken the night they flooded the rink. They looked like ice monsters. The caption said: **TO MY EXTREMELY COOL FRIEND — IT'S SNOW NICE 2 KNOW U!**

Tom opened his mailbox, stuffed with cards. Mark gave him a large flaming letter C. *It's the Calgary Flames C*, thought Tom.

Stuart gave him a postcard covered in scribbles. It said: Thanks for not getting mad at my sister.

Jordan gave him a puzzle card:

Flames @ 6!

"Oh, man." Tom wanted to watch the Flames, but all he could think about were snowflakes falling by the millions. And that made him nervous. *What should I do? Friendship is not easy. It is not a no-brainer.*

Tom looked around the classroom. He liked Mrs. Wong. She said there would be a party and there was. She said "no mushy love stuff" and there wasn't. You could count on her. And you could count on Coach Howie. He always said, "Stay focused and try your best." And he tipped his cap to say, "Hang in there! Never give up!"

Suddenly, Tom knew exactly what to do.

Teamwork

Tom pushed hard on the shovel, lifted a heavy load and dumped it along the edge of the rink. If he multiplied the time it took to clear a short pathway by the amount of snow left, he'd be working till midnight. He took a deep breath and kept going. His friends were probably at Jack's by now.

BLEEP! BLEEP! rang Tom's walkie-talkie. "Turn around!" crackled Stuart.

Stuart, Mark and Jordan were at the edge of the park, waving their shovels in the air. "Attack!" they shouted, trudging toward the snow-covered rink. The four boys lined up their shovels. "Heave-ho!" They pushed and

shovelled down the centre of the rink. They realigned their equipment and made a path around the outside.

Mark sang, *"We're shovelling along, singing our song, side by side!"*

Tom stopped to catch his breath. "At the rate we're going, we'll be finished in time to watch the game!"

"Told ya," said Jordan, "on the puzzle. Flames at 6."

BLEEP! BLEEP! Tom paged his mom for a ride to Jack's house, then dug back into the snow. Before long, the rink was a perfect sheet of ice.

"We're done!" shouted Tom. "Just in time!" He held out his fist and everyone banged theirs on top.

"Hawks!" they cheered.

"Wow!" raved Tom, sliding his boots over the surface. "This ice is really nice. The team will love it!"

"Hey, where's your letter C? The one I gave you at school?" asked Mark. "We voted you Rink Rat Team Captain for the weekend! That's your captain's C!"

"Sometimes we don't mind an extra push, to get the job done," said Stuart.

Tom smiled from his boots up. He saw his mom pull up in the car and Mr. Watson come out of his house to talk to her. "Let's go! Quick! To Jack's house!" Tom said, and they raced across the park.

"Hi, boys!" Mr. Watson stared at their red faces. "I've been noticing how hard you've worked on this rink. You guys have done a great job!" He smiled. "I'm wondering . . . could you check out another rink with me? Right now?" He looked at Tom's mom. "If that's okay with you."

"Oh, sure. Tom loves rink work," said his mom. She smiled. "And the other moms said yes."

Tom glanced at his watch. The Flames game started in twenty minutes. They were doomed.

Flames at 6

The boys slumped in the seats of Mr. Watson's car. Tom sat in front, trying not to frown. They turned left. Headed north. Suddenly, they were in a giant traffic jam. The right-hand lane was bumper to bumper. "Wow," said Tom. "This rink must be really important."

"You betcha," said Mr. Watson, turning into the parking lot of the Saddledome. If it weren't for the seatbelts, the boys would have jumped right through the roof.

Mr. Watson led them to a ticket gate at the main entrance of the arena.

ZIPPP — their tickets were scanned.

"We're really here," said Jordan, pinching himself.

The lobby was buzzing. Nearly everyone was wearing red. "Hurry," said Mr. Watson. "We need to get right down to ice level."

Tom's head spun — taking in the program sellers, the crowd and the Zamboni as they filed down the stairs. When they were seated next to the ice, Mr. Watson said, "Okay, Rink Rats, tonight you get to watch someone else clean the ice!"

The lights went out.

POOF! Two torches ignited, one above each net.

"Ladies and Gentlemen, your Calgary Flames!" boomed the announcer. A ring of fake fire circled the Saddledome as the players launched onto the ice. Spotlights zeroed in on their faces as they zoomed into a high-powered skate.

"Ahhhhh!" shrieked Tom, Jordan, Mark and Stuart. "Go, Flames, go!"

BANG! BANG! Harvey the Hound, the Flames' mascot, pounded his drum. "Arrooooo!" he howled.

Then Sidney Crosby stepped onto the ice.

Tom stood up. His jaw dropped and his knees weakened. He pressed his hands on the glass to keep his balance. Then, to his surprise, Sidney Crosby skated right in front of him, his jersey brushing the other side of the glass.

"Oh, man!" Tom gasped, blown away.

"He's awesome!" The players skated into a line and removed their helmets. When the crowd stood and sang "O Canada," Tom and his friends didn't miss a word.

As Tom took his seat, he couldn't help thinking how much he loved hockey, especially with his friends. A warm feeling tingled inside.

"Now, smile for the camera!" said Mr. Watson, pointing to the TV crew.

Tom and his friends waved.

"Hi, Mom!"

"Hi, Dad!"

"Hi, Hawks!"

Then Tom took a good look at the cameraman's cap. It was the same as Mr. Watson's. He nudged Stuart and pointed.

"Hey!" said Stuart. "I remember. You work for the television station!"

"Well, yes, I do." Mr. Watson winked. "And that gives me some special privileges."

On the way home, Jordan held the game puck in his hands, as if it were made of gold. Mark kissed his Flames ticket. Stuart kissed a photo of the Stanley Cup in his program. Tom hugged his jersey. It was plastered with autographs, including Sidney Crosby's.

Family Day

Monday, February 15. No school. It was Family Day!

Tom opened his front door and grabbed the newspaper. He checked out the weather forecast, then looked at the sky. A mild chinook wind was blowing through Calgary. It would warm up the day, but not enough to melt the rink into a giant slush drink.

———— • ————

One o'clock. Crescent Park.

As Tom, Stuart and Mark made one final ice check, Jordan set up the nets.

"I can't wait for the opening faceoff!" Tom shouted.

Coach Howie arrived at the rink, carrying cases of energy drinks. Then the Hawks landed. Jack brought popcorn. Zeke brought a barbecue. Ben brought hotdogs. Kyle and Nat brought music. And Spencer brought a cake that said Happy Family Day!

As the team put up balloons, streamers

and a giant Hawks flag, more cars pulled up, spilling out families. They unloaded lawn chairs, blankets, skate bags and hockey gear. Kaitlyn came across the road with Mr. Watson and a new hockey stick. "I'm ready for a hat trick!" she hollered.

After laces got tightened and helmets fastened, everyone gathered at the edge of the ice.

"This rink is great!" boomed Coach Howie.

"Superb job, Rink Rats!" agreed Mr. Watson. He winked at the boys and sat down on the bench.

"Woo hoo!" crowed the Hawks, and everyone clapped.

Tom and his friends leaned on their sticks, smiling proudly.

"Now, let's play hockey!" Coach Howie announced. "Game on!"

If you liked this book, look for these other books about Tom and his friends.

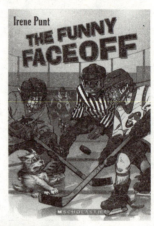

by Irene Punt